The Magic of Old St. Nick

THE ADVENTURE BEGINS

Written by Susan Gravely
Illustrated by Alessandro Taddei

Published by Vietri, Hillsborough, North Carolina

Edited by Brette Baumhover, Holli Draughn, and Natalie Riddick,
Vietri, Hillsborough, North Carolina

Book and cover design by Mollie Baker, Vietri, Hillsborough, North Carolina

Printed and bound in South Korea

Library of Congress Control Number: 2018939492

ISBN 978-1-7321133-0-5

10 9 8 7 6 5 4 3

A special thanks to Bill Ross for his endless hours, unfailing support,
and constant guidance.

Thank you to Susan McDonald, McDonald & Associates

For more information on Old St. Nick and Vietri, visit:
www.vietri.com

 DEDICATION

To our families, colleagues, and friends who
believe in the magic of Old St. Nick and have made
his adventures part of their holiday traditions.

In Italy a baby boy
Arrived and brought
his parents joy.

His cheeks were pink,
his eyes were bright,
His parents loved him
at first sight.

They called him
Nick for Nicholas,
A nickname like
his dad's, it was.

Said Dad,
"He will be gentle too;
A caring heart will
guide Nick through."

Nick crawled, then walked, and talked and laughed.

He played outside,

then took a bath.

He dreamed
of happy things
all night,

And woke each day
with great delight.

3

4

Babbo was what Nick
called his dad,
Two Nicks together –
both were glad!

The young boy watched
his dad make toys
To give to all good girls
and boys.

Babbo worked hard,
from toys to stable,
Nick pitched in as he was able.

6

"I'll feed the deer,
you load the sleigh –

Good job, my boy,"
Babbo did say.

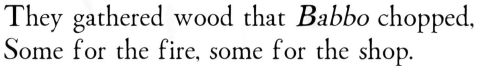

They gathered wood that *Babbo* chopped,
Some for the fire, some for the shop.

8

Everywhere that
Nick did go,
A red bird came
to let him know

That his dear
mother loved him so,
Tho' she had died
some years ago.

He'd make a friend or cut a tree –
The bird was there for him to see.

The red bird brought
him love and cheer
From those who loved
him, far and near.

Days passed by,
as years did too.
Nick helped his dad
with work to do.

He carved a boat,
he made a doll;
His love was making
gifts for all.

12

He heard his *Babbo*
say so clear,
"These *regali* - toys -
will bring much cheer."

When *Babbo* was all set to go,
Nick said,
"Be safe and please go slow!"

14

Nick thought of
Babbo's special flight,
And wished he, too,
could ride this night.

15

After
countless
'round-the-
world trips,
Babbo grew
old for
chimney dips.

He gently stroked his beard so white
And said to Nick, "The time is right.

Here are my hat, and coat, and gloves;
Wear them for me as you fly above."

17

The new St. Nick stepped up and said,
"*Babbo*, I'll lead as you have led.

From house to house, deliver toys,
Far and wide, to good girls and boys.

Please tell me, *Babbo,* how to do
This job that's meant so much to you?"

"Read your letters, start work early,
Make good toys, and do not hurry!

This is the night that you will fly
From house to house, and this is why:

The children sleep and dream of you,
Hoping their wishes might come true."

Years have passed
since the clock did tick,
And the bright-eyed child
became Old St. Nick.

23

So, children, know
he looks for you
To do your best,
be good and true,

Be kind to all,
help those with needs,

And spread your love
with your good deeds.

With job well done,
Nick sat to rest.
He gathered his gifts
and wore his best.

Tonight, with friends
and family too,
Buon Natale to all!
Merry Christmas
to you!

29

Glossary

1. **Babbo** *(bàh-bo)* What many Italians, especially in Tuscany, call their father.

2. **Buon Natale!** *(bwon na-ta-lay)* Italian for Merry Christmas!

3. **Casa Dolce Casa** *(cà-za dol-che cà-za)* Italian for Home Sweet Home.

4. **Dormi bene** *(door-me beh-neh)* Italian for Sleep well.

5. **Regali** *(re-gal-ee)* Italian for Gifts.

6. **The story of the red berries.**

   The number of red berries worn in the caps of Nick and Old St. Nick symbolize their maturity and life experiences.

7. **The story of the red bird.**

   The red bird is an international symbol signifying the presence of friends and family members who are watching over you with love and affection.